ROWAN AVA SKYE

The Axolotl's Heartwarming Quest

Copyright © 2024 by Rowan Ava Skye

All rights reserved. No part of this publication may be reproduced, stored or transmitted in any form or by any means, electronic, mechanical, photocopying, recording, scanning, or otherwise without written permission from the publisher. It is illegal to copy this book, post it to a website, or distribute it by any other means without permission.

This novel is entirely a work of fiction. The names, characters and incidents portrayed in it are the work of the author's imagination. Any resemblance to actual persons, living or dead, events or localities is entirely coincidental.

First edition

ISBN: 9798301170126

This book was professionally typeset on Reedsy. Find out more at reedsy.com

Contents

Introduction	1
Chapter 1: A Clue in the Current	2
Chapter 2: The Glow of Friendship	5
Chapter 3: The Whirlpool of Courage	8
Chapter 4: The Labyrinth of Trust	11
Chapter 5: The Test of the Heart	15
Chapter 6: The Glow of Friendship	18
Afterword	21

Introduction

Welcome to the whimsical world of *The Axolotl's Heartwarming Quest*, where magic, friendship, and adventure swim hand in hand!

Meet Axel, a curious and brave axolotl who lives in a colorful underwater village filled with wonder and surprises. When a mysterious darkness threatens to dim the light and love in his home, Axel must embark on an extraordinary journey to restore it. Along the way, he discovers that true magic lies not in treasure but in the bonds we share and the courage to follow our hearts.

Join Axel and his bubbly sidekick, Petunia the playful crab, as they face daring challenges, unlock enchanted secrets, and learn the greatest lesson of all: that love and kindness can light up even the darkest depths.

So, dive in and let your imagination soar in this enchanting Valentine's Day adventure that will warm your heart and leave you smiling from start to finish!

Chapter 1: A Clue in the Current

A xel woke up to a world brimming with possibilities. The gentle ripples of Coral Cove's lagoon reflected the dawn light, painting the water in shades of pink, orange, and gold. It was a special morning; Valentine's Day was just around the corner. The entire lagoon seemed alive with excitement.

Every corner of Coral Cove bustled with activity. Sea cucumbers rolled by, delivering baskets of rose-colored algae treats to neighbors. Starfish hung heart-shaped kelp garlands from coral spires. Even the shy seahorses peered out from their hideaways, ready to join the festivities.

Yet, as Axel swam through the vibrant scene, a nagging feeling tugged at his heart. Unlike his neighbors, Axel didn't have a gift to give. He wanted something extraordinary—something that would make his friends and family feel truly loved.

Later that day, Axel visited Grandma Coral, the wise old turtle who always seemed to have the perfect advice. Her shell was adorned with barnacle carvings that told stories of the ocean's history.

"Grandma Coral," Axel began, his voice tinged with uncertainty, "I want to give everyone in Coral Cove a gift for Valentine's Day. But not just any gift—something that shows them how much they mean to me. Do you think there's such a thing?"

Grandma Coral smiled warmly, her eyes twinkling like sunlight on the

Chapter 1: A Clue in the Current

water. "Ah, Axel, your heart is as big as the sea. There is a gift like that, but it's not one you can buy or find easily. It's said that somewhere in these waters lies a treasure—one that embodies the truest form of love: kindness, courage, and joy."

Axel's gills fluttered with excitement. "A treasure? Where can I find it?"

Grandma Coral chuckled. "That, my dear, is a question only you can answer. The treasure is hidden deep within the ocean. Its path is marked by challenges, but the journey itself holds lessons that will guide you. Only a heart like yours can uncover it."

As the sun dipped below the horizon, casting the lagoon in a silvery glow, Axel lay in his favorite nook within a coral alcove. The idea of a treasure quest filled his mind, and as he drifted to sleep, dreams of adventure swirled around him.

The next morning, Axel awoke with newfound determination. "This Valentine's Day," he declared to himself, "I will find the treasure and give everyone in Coral Cove a gift they'll never forget!"

With a final glance at the bustling cove, Axel swam out into the open ocean. The waters beyond Coral Cove were uncharted territory for him—a vast expanse of mystery and wonder.

Not long into his journey, Axel noticed something unusual. A soft, golden light shimmered in the distance, pulsating like a heartbeat. Drawn to its glow, Axel swam closer, weaving through forests of kelp and fields of swaying seaweed.

Nestled among the rocks was an ancient conch shell, its surface etched with intricate patterns that seemed to shimmer in the light. Curious, Axel picked up the shell and held it close. To his astonishment, a melodic voice emanated from within:

"To find the treasure, follow the light, Through twists and turns, both left and right. Seek the creature with a heart so true, They'll guide the way with a riddle or two."

Axel's heart raced with excitement. "Follow the light," he repeated, scanning the waters around him. Sure enough, a faint golden glow flickered in the distance.

Without hesitation, Axel swam toward the light. The journey led him through a maze-like kelp forest, where the currents twisted and turned unpredictably. The deeper he ventured, the more the forest seemed alive, with strands of kelp reaching out like curious fingers.

Suddenly, Axel found his path blocked by a school of puffers. Each one puffed up like a spiky balloon, creating an impenetrable wall.

"Where do you think you're going?" one of them asked, its voice gruff but not unkind.

"I'm on a quest to find the treasure of love and kindness," Axel replied earnestly.

The puffers exchanged amused glances. "A noble goal," said the leader of the group. "But if you want to pass, you'll need to prove your worth. Solve our riddle, and we'll let you through."

The puffers spun in a synchronized dance, forming shapes in the water. At last, they paused, their movements creating a pattern that resembled a heart.

"Here is your riddle," the leader declared. "What has no beginning, no end, and binds us all together?"

Axel paused, tapping a tiny toe against a nearby rock. He thought about the treasures Grandma Coral had mentioned: kindness, courage, joy. Then it hit him.

"It's love!" Axel exclaimed. "Love has no end and connects us all."

The puffers deflated with surprise, their spikes retreating. "Correct!" they chorused, parting to reveal the path ahead.

As Axel swam past them, the golden light grew brighter, and the sense of adventure swelled in his chest. He didn't know what challenges lay ahead, but he felt ready to face them. After all, the treasure he sought wasn't just for him—it was for everyone he cared about.

Chapter 2: The Glow of Friendship

The ocean beyond Coral Cove seemed endless, stretching out in a dazzling display of blue and green. The deeper Axel swam, the more the world around him transformed. The coral beds gave way to mysterious, towering kelp forests that swayed like graceful dancers in the current. Streams of sunlight pierced the water, casting golden patterns on the ocean floor.

Axel felt a mix of excitement and unease. He had never been this far from home before, and the vastness of the open ocean made him feel very small. But the memory of Grandma Coral's words about the treasure kept him moving forward.

It wasn't long before Axel spotted something curious—a cluster of rocks forming an archway that led into a shadowy expanse. Above the arch, small fish darted back and forth, creating tiny sparkles like fireflies. Axel hesitated. The glowing light he had been following seemed to lead straight through the arch.

"Here goes nothing," Axel murmured to himself, summoning his courage as he swam forward.

As he passed under the archway, a new world opened before him. He found himself in a vast underwater meadow unlike anything he had ever seen. The ground was carpeted with soft, pink seagrass, and heart-shaped flowers of every shade of red and pink swayed gently in the current. Tiny bubbles floated lazily upward, reflecting the colors of the meadow like miniature rainbows.

Axel's eyes widened in wonder. "This must be a magical place," he whispered.

But before he could explore further, a soft, melodic humming reached his ears. It was a sweet, cheerful tune that seemed to make the water around him shimmer. Curious, Axel followed the sound, weaving through the meadow until he came upon a rock covered in moss.

Sitting on the rock was a tiny snail with a shimmering shell that glowed faintly in the dim light. The snail was humming happily, oblivious to Axel's presence.

"Hello there," Axel called gently, not wanting to startle the snail.

The snail stopped humming and looked up, her eyes widening in surprise. "Oh! Hello! I didn't see you there," she said, her voice as soft as the tune she had been humming. "I'm Petunia. Who might you be?"

"I'm Axel," he replied with a polite bow. "I'm on a quest to find a treasure that symbolizes love and kindness. Have you seen a glowing light pass through here?"

Petunia's antennae twitched thoughtfully. "A glowing light, you say? I've seen many lights, but the one you're seeking sounds very special. Tell me more."

Axel explained his mission, describing the treasure and the riddle he had solved to get this far. As he spoke, Petunia listened intently, her shimmering shell catching the light with every small movement.

When he finished, Petunia nodded slowly. "Your quest sounds important, Axel, and I'd like to help you. The treasure you seek won't be easy to find, but every journey is better with a friend, don't you think?"

Axel smiled brightly. "I couldn't agree more. I'd love for you to join me!"

With a happy squeal, Petunia slid down from her rock and onto the seagrass beside Axel. Though she was small and slow, her determination made her glow even brighter.

Together, they set off across the meadow, their path lit by the faint golden light that Axel had been following. As they moved, Petunia pointed out hidden wonders Axel might have missed—a cluster of tiny, glowing jellyfish, a family

Chapter 2: The Glow of Friendship

of seahorses playing in the grass, and a patch of coral shaped like a heart.

"Magic is everywhere," Petunia said softly, "but only those with kind hearts can truly see it."

Their journey soon brought them to the center of the meadow, where a large sea urchin rested on the ocean floor. Its spines were long and sharp, forming a protective barrier around something glowing faintly beneath it. Axel and Petunia stopped a few paces away, their curiosity piqued.

"That must be part of the treasure!" Axel whispered.

As they approached, the sea urchin stirred, its spines shifting slightly. A deep, rumbling voice echoed from within. "Who dares disturb my sanctuary?"

Axel stepped forward bravely. "I'm Axel, and this is my friend Petunia. We're on a quest to find a treasure that embodies love and kindness. May we pass?"

The sea urchin's spines quivered, and its voice softened. "To pass, you must prove your worth. Show me an act of true kindness, and the path will be revealed."

Axel and Petunia exchanged a puzzled glance. What could they do to demonstrate kindness? As they thought, a small fish darted into view. It seemed panicked, thrashing wildly as it tried to free itself from a tangled strand of seaweed caught on the sea urchin's spines.

"Hold still," Axel said gently to the fish, swimming closer. With careful movements, he untangled the seaweed, freeing the frightened fish. The fish swam in circles around Axel before darting off with a sparkle of gratitude.

The sea urchin's spines relaxed, parting to reveal a glowing pearl nestled at its center. "You have shown kindness," the sea urchin rumbled. "Take this pearl as a token of your journey, and may it guide you to the treasure you seek."

Axel picked up the pearl, its warmth radiating through his fins. He smiled at Petunia, who beamed with pride. Together, they continued their journey, the glowing light ahead calling them forward.

Chapter 3: The Whirlpool of Courage

The ocean grew darker and colder as Axel and Petunia journeyed farther from the vibrant meadow. The pearl Axel carried glowed softly, lighting their path as they ventured into the unknown. The faint golden light they had been following flickered ahead, weaving through the murky waters like a will-o'-the-wisp.

Petunia, perched on Axel's back, shivered slightly. "Do you think we're getting close to the treasure?" she asked, her voice a mixture of curiosity and nervousness.

"I hope so," Axel replied, his tone steady. "But Grandma Coral said the journey would be full of challenges. We've shown kindness; now, we'll have to see what's next."

As they swam on, the current began to shift. What had been a gentle, flowing stream of water turned into a stronger, swirling force. Axel noticed the sand on the ocean floor being pulled in spirals, creating patterns that led to a massive whirlpool ahead.

The whirlpool churned violently, its edges frothing with bubbles. In its center, the faint golden glow pulsed like a heartbeat, calling to them. Axel stopped a short distance away, staring at the powerful current.

"That's… a bit intimidating," Petunia admitted, clutching tightly to Axel's back.

Axel took a deep breath. "We've come this far, Petunia. We can't turn back

Chapter 3: The Whirlpool of Courage

now. The light is in there—we have to go through."

Petunia hesitated but then nodded. "You're right. Let's be brave together."

With a determined flick of his tail, Axel propelled them closer to the whirlpool. The force of the current grew stronger, tugging at them with increasing intensity. Axel had to focus all his energy on swimming straight, his fins straining against the pull.

"Hold on tight!" Axel called to Petunia, who squeaked in response, wrapping herself snugly around his back.

As they entered the whirlpool, the world around them became a blur. The water roared in their ears, and the spinning current made it difficult to see. Axel's muscles burned with effort, but he pressed on, guided by the golden glow at the center.

Suddenly, a deep, resonant voice boomed through the chaos. "Who dares to enter the Whirlpool of Courage?"

Axel paused, his heart racing. "I'm Axel, and this is my friend Petunia! We're on a quest to find the treasure of love and kindness."

The voice rumbled with amusement. "Courage is the key to progress, young adventurers. But courage is not the absence of fear—it is the triumph over it. To pass through, you must face your greatest fear. Do you accept the challenge?"

Axel swallowed hard. "I accept," he said firmly, though his voice wavered slightly.

"And what about you, little one?" the voice asked Petunia.

Petunia trembled but found her voice. "I accept, too. We'll face it together!"

The whirlpool suddenly calmed, the spinning slowing just enough for Axel and Petunia to regain their bearings. Then, the water around them began to shimmer, and a strange scene unfolded.

In the swirling depths of the whirlpool, images appeared like reflections in a mirror. Axel gasped as he saw a shadowy version of Coral Cove—a version where everything was eerily silent, the vibrant colors faded to dull grays. His friends and family floated motionlessly, their faces void of joy or life.

"No," Axel whispered, his heart aching. "That's my greatest fear—losing everyone I care about, and not being able to make them happy."

Petunia's reflection appeared beside his, showing her clinging to her rock, alone in a vast, empty ocean. "I... I'm afraid of being forgotten," she admitted softly.

The booming voice returned. "Your fears are powerful, but they are only illusions. Courage will guide you to the truth. Will you confront them, or will you turn back?"

Axel's mind raced. The sight of Coral Cove devoid of joy was almost too much to bear. But he reminded himself of the kindness he had already shown, of the pearl in his possession, and of the golden light that had guided him this far.

"I won't let fear stop me," Axel said, his voice gaining strength. "I'll keep going, no matter what!"

Petunia clung to his back, her tiny voice steady. "Me too! I'll never give up!"

As they spoke, the images began to waver, their edges dissolving into shimmering bubbles. The booming voice returned, softer this time. "You have faced your fears with courage and truth. The whirlpool will no longer hold you."

The current around them stilled, and the golden glow grew brighter, illuminating a pathway ahead. Axel and Petunia swam forward, their hearts lighter than before.

On the other side of the whirlpool, they emerged into a tranquil lagoon. The water here was crystal clear, and the golden light bathed everything in a warm, soothing glow. In the center of the lagoon stood a coral pedestal, upon which rested a second pearl—this one glowing with a vibrant, fiery orange hue.

Petunia gasped in awe. "It's beautiful!"

Axel swam to the pedestal and picked up the pearl. As soon as it touched his fins, a wave of warmth spread through him, filling him with confidence and resolve. He smiled at Petunia, who beamed back at him.

"Two pearls," Axel said, his voice filled with determination. "We're getting closer, Petunia. The treasure is within reach—I can feel it!"

With the second pearl in hand, Axel and Petunia set off once more, ready to face whatever challenges lay ahead.

Chapter 4: The Labyrinth of Trust

After leaving the tranquil lagoon, Axel and Petunia continued their journey through the glowing depths of the ocean. The warmth from the two pearls—one blue and one orange—guided them forward, their soft glow lighting the way as the ocean floor shifted beneath them.

Axel couldn't help but feel a growing sense of pride. Two challenges down, and while they were difficult, they had proven that kindness and courage could overcome anything. Petunia, perched on his back, seemed equally determined, though her usual chatter had quieted as they swam into an unfamiliar territory.

Ahead, the seascape changed drastically. What had been a gently sloping seabed transformed into towering coral walls, their surfaces covered with anemones and swaying kelp. The passage narrowed, leading them into a twisting maze of coral corridors that seemed to stretch endlessly.

"This… doesn't look straightforward," Petunia said, her small voice echoing off the walls.

"It's a labyrinth," Axel said, a mix of awe and apprehension in his tone. "We just have to find the right path."

As they swam deeper, the golden light they had been following split into multiple trails, each glowing faintly as it wound through the maze. Axel hesitated, unsure which to follow.

"Do we choose one?" Petunia asked, tilting her head.

Before Axel could answer, a melodious but eerie voice filled the labyrinth. "Ah, travelers! Welcome to the Labyrinth of Trust. To find your way through, you must rely on something greater than sight. Do you trust yourselves... and each other?"

Axel felt a shiver run down his spine. The voice was soft, almost soothing, but its challenge was clear. "We do trust each other," Axel said firmly.

"Very well," the voice replied. "But trust is not just a word. It is an action, a bond, a leap of faith. Follow the light of trust, but beware—this labyrinth is not without tricks. False paths lead to confusion, and only true trust will reveal the way."

Axel exchanged a glance with Petunia, her small eyes wide with uncertainty. "I guess we just have to... pick a path and trust it's the right one?"

Petunia nodded slowly. "But how will we know it's the right one? What if it's a trick?"

Axel considered this for a moment, then smiled. "We'll figure it out together. If one path doesn't work, we'll try another. We've made it this far, haven't we?"

His words seemed to reassure Petunia, and together they swam toward the first glowing trail. The path led them deeper into the labyrinth, the coral walls growing tighter around them. The silence was heavy, broken only by the gentle swish of their movements.

But as they reached the end of the trail, the golden glow faded, leaving them in dim light. The path had been a dead end.

"Oh no," Petunia said, her voice tinged with disappointment.

"It's okay," Axel replied, turning them around. "We'll try the next one. We just have to stay calm and trust we'll find the right way."

The second path seemed more promising at first. The golden light brightened, and the walls of the labyrinth opened into a larger chamber. But as they entered, a sudden rush of water trapped them in a swirling vortex, spinning them in circles.

Axel fought against the current, his fins working tirelessly until they broke free. "Another trick," he panted, his chest heaving. "This labyrinth isn't going to make it easy, is it?"

Chapter 4: The Labyrinth of Trust

"No," Petunia said softly, "but maybe we're missing something." She pointed a tiny claw at the two pearls Axel carried. "The pearls are supposed to help us, right? Maybe they're the key."

Axel nodded thoughtfully. "You're right. Let's try focusing on the pearls."

He held the blue and orange pearls tightly, their combined glow casting a warm, calming light. As he swam toward the third path, he noticed something different. The golden trail on this path pulsed faintly, in sync with the glow of the pearls.

"This has to be it," Axel said, his voice filled with hope.

As they followed the path, the labyrinth began to shift around them. Walls moved, corridors opened, and the way ahead became clearer. It was as if the pearls were guiding them, responding to their trust and determination.

The melodic voice returned, softer this time. "You are learning well, young adventurers. Trust is not only in the path you choose but in each other and in the journey itself."

Petunia smiled, her confidence growing. "We're doing it, Axel! We're really doing it!"

Finally, the labyrinth opened into a grand chamber, its walls shimmering with golden light. In the center stood a pedestal made of crystal-clear coral, upon which rested the third pearl. This one glowed with a soft green hue, radiating a sense of peace and balance.

Axel and Petunia swam to the pedestal, their hearts swelling with accomplishment. Axel reached out and gently took the green pearl, feeling a soothing warmth spread through him.

"This one feels… different," Axel said, marveling at the pearl's glow. "It's like it's reminding us to stay calm and trust the journey, no matter what."

Petunia nodded. "I think it's teaching us to trust ourselves and each other, even when things get tough."

As they left the chamber, the labyrinth shifted one final time, creating a straight path leading back to the open ocean. Axel and Petunia swam forward, the three pearls glowing brightly in their fins.

"Three pearls," Axel said, his voice filled with determination. "We're getting closer, Petunia. I can feel it!"

Petunia beamed. "And no matter what comes next, I trust we can handle it together."

Chapter 5: The Test of the Heart

Axel and Petunia emerged from the labyrinth into a serene, moonlit ocean. Above them, the water shimmered with soft silvery light, while below, the seafloor sparkled with bioluminescent flora. The three pearls they had collected—blue, orange, and green—glowed faintly in Axel's fins, their combined light creating a kaleidoscope of colors in the water.

"This place is beautiful," Petunia said in awe, her voice almost a whisper.

Axel nodded, but a sense of unease prickled at him. Each trial so far had pushed them to their limits, and he suspected the next one would be no different. Still, they had come too far to turn back now.

As they swam farther, a soft humming filled the water, growing louder with each stroke. Ahead of them stood a large archway carved from coral, its surface covered in intricate heart-shaped patterns. The pearls in Axel's fins began to vibrate slightly, their glow intensifying as they neared the arch.

"This must be it," Axel said, his voice steady despite the butterflies in his stomach. "The fourth trial."

They passed through the arch, and the world around them shifted. The ocean faded away, replaced by a shimmering, dreamlike landscape. Axel and Petunia now stood on a soft, sandy path surrounded by blooming flowers and glowing hearts that floated lazily through the air. The scene was warm and inviting, but Axel knew better than to let his guard down.

"Welcome, travelers," said a deep, resonant voice. Axel and Petunia turned to see a majestic seahorse with a golden mane and shimmering scales. It floated gracefully before them, its eyes filled with wisdom. "You have proven your courage, kindness, and trust. But the final trial is the Test of the Heart. Are you ready?"

Axel stepped forward, holding his head high. "We're ready."

The seahorse nodded. "Very well. This test will reveal the strength of your heart and the choices you make when faced with the unexpected. Follow me."

The seahorse led them to a large clearing where a glowing heart-shaped crystal hovered in the air. It pulsed gently, its light filling the space with warmth. Surrounding the crystal were three paths, each leading in a different direction.

"To complete this trial, you must choose the path that reflects the true desires of your heart," the seahorse explained. "But beware, not all paths lead to your destination. Some may lead to challenges, others to distractions. Choose wisely."

Axel and Petunia exchanged a glance. "How do we know which path is the right one?" Petunia asked, her voice tinged with worry.

"The heart knows," the seahorse replied simply.

Axel approached the crystal, his fins tingling as its light washed over him. The three paths glowed faintly: the first with a fiery red light, the second with a calming blue, and the third with a soft golden hue.

"I think the red one represents passion," Axel said, studying the paths. "The blue feels peaceful, and the gold... maybe that's about love or hope."

Petunia nodded thoughtfully. "But which one should we take?"

Axel closed his eyes, letting the warmth of the crystal guide him. Images began to form in his mind—his parents smiling proudly, his friends cheering him on, the glowing heart-shaped tree from his dreams. He realized that each path represented a different part of his journey, but only one reflected the reason he had started this quest: to bring love and joy back to his village.

"The golden path," Axel said confidently. "It's the one that feels right."

Petunia trusted him completely and followed as Axel stepped onto the golden path. The world around them shifted again, and they found themselves in a vast meadow filled with dazzling lights. The heart-shaped tree from Axel's

Chapter 5: The Test of the Heart

visions stood tall in the center, its branches glowing with an otherworldly light.

"We did it!" Petunia exclaimed, her tiny claws clapping together in delight.

But as they approached the tree, a shadowy figure emerged from its base. It was a large eel-like creature, its eyes glowing with malice. "So, you think you can just take the tree's gift and leave?" it hissed. "Not without proving you are worthy!"

Axel's heart pounded, but he stepped forward bravely. "We've faced every challenge and shown kindness, courage, and trust. What more do we need to prove?"

The eel circled them, its body shimmering ominously. "The greatest test of all: sacrifice. To claim the tree's gift, one of you must stay behind, forever guarding its light."

Petunia gasped. "But... that's not fair!"

Axel felt a lump in his throat. The thought of leaving Petunia or giving up his dream was unbearable. But he also knew what his heart was telling him.

"If it means saving my village," Axel said quietly, "I'll stay."

"No!" Petunia cried, her voice trembling. "We can't leave without you, Axel. There has to be another way!"

The eel grinned. "Such noble words. But sacrifices are not always what they seem." It disappeared in a swirl of darkness, and the tree's light grew brighter, enveloping Axel and Petunia.

When the light faded, Axel found himself holding a glowing heart-shaped fruit in his fins. The tree stood taller and more vibrant than ever, its branches reaching toward the heavens.

"You have proven your worth," the seahorse's voice echoed. "The greatest strength of the heart is the willingness to give, even at great personal cost. Take the tree's gift and share its light with the world."

Axel turned to Petunia, who was beaming with pride. "We did it," he said, his voice filled with emotion. "Together."

Chapter 6: The Glow of Friendship

The journey back to the village was filled with a quiet sense of triumph. Axel and Petunia swam side by side, the glowing heart-shaped fruit cradled carefully in Axel's fins. Its light wasn't just warm—it radiated something deeper, something that filled both of them with a renewed sense of hope and purpose.

"Do you think this will work?" Petunia asked, her voice a mix of curiosity and wonder.

Axel glanced at the fruit and smiled. "I think it already has."

As they swam closer to the village, they noticed how quiet it had become. The once vibrant coral homes were dim, and the ocean floor seemed to lack the lively bustle they remembered. The gloom that had overtaken the village was heavier than ever.

But when the first villager spotted them, a ripple of excitement spread through the water. One by one, the villagers gathered, their faces lighting up at the sight of Axel and Petunia.

"Axel! You're back!" Benny the blowfish called, puffing up in excitement.

"And what is that you're holding?" asked Coral, the wise old sea turtle, her deep eyes twinkling.

Axel held up the glowing fruit for everyone to see. "This is the Heart of Light," he announced. "It's a gift from the heart-shaped tree in the enchanted forest. Its glow carries the magic of love and friendship. With it, we can bring

Chapter 6: The Glow of Friendship

the light back to our village."

The villagers exchanged astonished glances, their excitement growing.

"How does it work?" Benny asked.

Axel looked at the fruit, then at Petunia. "The seahorse said the greatest strength of the heart is the willingness to give. I think this fruit's light is meant to be shared."

Petunia nodded. "It's like a ripple in the water. A single drop can spread far and wide."

Axel held the fruit high and closed his eyes, letting its warmth guide him. Slowly, the fruit began to glow brighter, its light radiating outward in soft, shimmering waves. The villagers gasped as the light reached them, wrapping around each of them like a gentle hug.

Suddenly, the village came alive. The coral homes sparkled with vibrant colors, and the once-dim ocean floor glowed with bioluminescent life. The villagers' faces were filled with joy and a renewed sense of connection.

"It's beautiful," Coral said, her voice thick with emotion.

Axel turned to Petunia, his smile wide and genuine. "We did it."

But the fruit wasn't finished yet. To Axel's surprise, the light began to form heart-shaped bubbles that floated upward, spreading beyond the village. It was as if the magic of the tree wanted to share its gift with the entire ocean.

Over the following days, the village transformed. Neighbors helped one another with their daily tasks, shared stories, and celebrated their renewed sense of unity. Axel noticed how even the smallest acts of kindness seemed to carry a special glow, as if the fruit's magic had embedded itself into their hearts.

On the day of the big celebration, the villagers gathered in the center of the village, where a heart-shaped monument had been built to honor Axel and Petunia's journey.

"You've reminded us of what truly matters," Coral said as she presented Axel with a garland of glowing flowers. "It's not just about the light; it's about the love and friendship that sustain it."

Axel felt his cheeks flush with pride, but he quickly gestured toward Petunia. "I couldn't have done it without Petunia. She's the real hero."

Petunia giggled, her tiny claws waving dismissively. "Oh, stop it, Axel. You're making me blush!"

As the celebration continued, Axel looked around at his friends and neighbors. The journey had been long and filled with challenges, but it had brought them closer than ever. He realized that the real treasure wasn't the fruit or even the light—it was the bonds they had strengthened along the way.

Later that evening, Axel and Petunia sat together on a coral ledge, watching the heart-shaped bubbles drift off into the distance. The ocean was alive with color and light, a living testament to the magic of the Heart of Light.

"What do you think is out there?" Petunia asked, her voice soft and dreamy.

"Who knows?" Axel replied, his eyes twinkling. "But whatever it is, I know we'll face it together."

As the glowing bubbles floated into the horizon, Axel felt a sense of peace he had never known before. The Heart of Light had not only restored the village—it had changed him. He understood now that the greatest adventures weren't about finding treasure but about discovering the strength and love within oneself.

And as he sat there, surrounded by his closest friend and the warmth of the village's newfound light, Axel knew this was only the beginning of many more adventures to come.

Afterword

Thank you so much for joining Axel and Petunia on their magical journey in *The Axolotl's Heartwarming Quest*. This tale is a reminder of the strength found in friendship, courage, and the joy of spreading love to others. Your support and imagination help bring these stories to life, and I'm so grateful to have shared this adventure with you.

Stay tuned, because this is just the beginning! In the coming days, get ready for another thrilling adventure in the enchanted ocean with *Axel and Petunia's Coral Treasure Mystery*. This new story will dive deeper into the wonders of their world, uncovering hidden secrets and introducing exciting new characters.

If you enjoyed this story, be sure to check out the other enchanting tales by Rowan Ava Skye. Each book in the series is filled with heart, adventure, and a little touch of magic, perfect for readers young and old.

Your love for these stories inspires us to continue creating, so thank you for being part of this journey. Until next time, keep exploring, dreaming, and spreading the magic of love and kindness wherever you go.

With warmest wishes,
Rowan Ava Skye

Made in United States
Troutdale, OR
05/01/2025